HOME RUN

HOME RUN

William Aiello

ARPress
ILLUMINATING IDEAS,
EMPOWERING VOICES

ARPress LLC
45 Dan Road Suite 5
Canton MA 02021
Hotline: 1(888) 821-0229
Fax: 1(508) 545-7580

Ordering Information:
Quantity sales. Special discounts are available on quantity purchases by corporations, associations, and others. For details, contact the publisher at the address above.

Printed in the United States of America.

ISBN-13:   Softcover   979-8-89330-043-7
                eBook   979-8-89330-044-4

Library of Congress Control Number: 2024900565

Dedicated to Concettina Aiello
"And that's the whole thing."

CONTENTS

Chapter I 1

Chapter II 4

Chapter III 6

Chapter IV 9

Chapter V 13

Chapter VI 17

Chapter VII 18

Chapter VIII 19

Chapter IX 23

Chapter X 26

Chapter XI 29

CHAPTER 1

It was a day Bobby Campbell had waited weeks for. The first day of summer vacation and the first game his team was playing after school ended.

When he woke up that morning it was 78 degrees, rising rapidly and it was 87 degrees when he was getting ready to leave. The forecast was for close to 100 and it sure felt like it was coming soon.

The ballfield where he was playing today was in another part of town. Bobby's Uncle Chris was driving him and his cousin Wayne, also a member of the team. Bobby was overjoyed, it was the beginning of summer vacation, and looked like it was off to an exciting start.

He was thrilled in a way only a nine-year-old could be. Quickly he gulped down his breakfast despite his mother's admonition that he chew slower and not so much at a time.

But nothing else mattered at the moment. He wanted to have breakfast, don his uniform, and get going. The fact that his father couldn't take him because Dad got a promotion at the job, was working longer hours and the family might not go away this summer didn't matter. Nor did his oldest sister's elation that she got accepted to the college she was hoping to attend.

No, nothing else mattered. He wanted to get out to that ballfield and play his league game. And if it finished early, he knew he'd want to play another game.

After breakfast, got his uniform and equipment, and just as he finished Uncle Chris honked the horn and Bobby dashed outside. He beamed as Wayne told him to hurry and they were off in the car to a day he waited impatiently for.

When they got there, the boys practically jumped from the car and met the rest of the team preparing to play. This game was played in a remote part of town on a road where there was little traffic. No houses nearby, nor churches nor stores where they had to be careful about foul balls, noise or cars passing. Only a small, lonely, old cemetery, so old that hardly ever was anyone in there to respect their deceased loved ones.

It was surrounded by a wrought iron fence and high gates. Although a caretaker came around from time to time, the grounds and gravestones were seldom cared for. Weeds abounded, shrubs not pruned, and rarely any flowers at graves.

At nine years old, Bobby wasn't interested in an old graveyard. But had he looked he'd see the graves of veterans from the Civil War and the two world wars, early settlers of his county and dates from the 1700s to the mid-1900s. These people were long gone. And so, evidently, were their descendants.

And so infrequently did people come here, that there wasn't anyone to care full time for the grounds or grant admission. It was done with a key family had, and only once did Bobby hear a spectator at the ballgames inquire how could anyone get into the cemetery if the key was lost. But the cemetery stood almost without character or presence in a plot just yards away, yet which seemed to be entirely alone and solitary, completely separated from the flurry of activity at the ballfield.

The sun shone and beat down mightily as the temperature rose to 101. Bobby was having one of his best days ever, aided by the fact that his team was winning. So lively and active a day, and his team won the game. A short break, and they were going to play again. During the intermission practice, Bobby hit a ball way across the spectator stand into the graveyard. The coach, who had the supply of balls, had taken a ride away to lunch. So the ball had to be retrieved. Seemed like no way into the yard.

Leave it up to young boys to figure it out. There was a break in the fence around the rear of the cemetery plot, along the wooded area. Bobby and teammate Mike were able to squeeze through.   That was the easy part. What wasn't so simple was finding the ball. Some of the teammates and family members guided the boys to the general area where the ball landed. They hopped over weeds and branches. Adults told them to be careful for rodents and snakes known to be on the grounds. Walking back and forth, to and from, guided by people's perceptions as to where the ball might be. Finally someone saw it.

"There it is", yelled the mother of Glenn, a boy watching the search. In front of one of the smaller headstones. She couldn't quite make out the name, weeds partially covering it. Zacek or Zaszek or something similar. Trying her best to say the name properly, Bobby finally saw the name and found the ball. For just a second, he glanced at both the stone and the name, reached between thick weeds, and grabbed the ball.

Then he and Wayne charged back to the split in the fence where they came in. They were joined by Glenn and the other boys, another game about to begin. How little did Bobby Campbell know that decades later he'd remember that grave more lucidly than the two games his team triumphantly won.

CHAPTER II

It was 52 years since young Bobby's team won those two ball games. Bobby was now Bob, it was over half a century later, he was a detective. Married, with two grown children, one grandchild and another on the way. Ball games didn't mean much to him anymore. Work and family occupied his time. A detective over thirty years, he'd seen all kinds of cases and had all kinds of clients.

Coming into his office this day was detective Kevin Larson. Bob and Larson had been working together for over twenty years. Together they helped solve many crimes and in the course of investigations became good friends. They were like brothers.

Detective Larson came in to report the latest in a series of robberies on the west side of town. In every case the facts were the same: the victim came home to find the place ransacked and valuables stolen. The thief or thieves knew just where to go. Whether it was jewelry or money, cameras or stamp collections, coins or figurines, the booty was taken. No other parts of the homes were disturbed. The perpetrators went right in and right out.

The latest victim was Edith, a small, 70ish widow, who returned home from a night of Bingo. She walked in and found the dresser drawer open, jewelry all gone. It was the second robbery in her neighborhood in one week. Bob Campbell was quite upset. These robberies were not just throwing fear into citizens, but making his force appear bad. Looked like this time Campbell had better accompany Larson to the crime scene.

Detective Larson had just interviewed Edith, as well as a few neighbors. There was a trend. In each case the victims were out for a few hours. Edith went to Bingo. The criminal had to know she would not be home for a couple of hours. News of the robbery was reported by the local media and pressure was mounting on the police force. Get these guys or pretty soon there's going to be another robbery.

Larson carefully looked around Edith's home. In previous crimes there wasn't much evidence. Whoever was committing the robberies wasn't leaving any clues or evidence behind. This time, however, there was something. Caught on the fire escape was a small piece of cloth with a button. On the face of the button was a pool table and cue.

Both men studied it curiously and intently.

Could it mean the burglar was a pool shark?

The pool halls in town were known for being more social outlets than criminal hangouts. Or so they thought. But there existed the possibility that a pool player was committing these crimes. So Campbell and Larson had to figure a way to go inside and observe the players without drawing attention. Campbell felt two undercover cops could do the job. Campbell didn't have the right look. Even in plain clothes, he looked and acted too much like a detective. Plus he admitted to being a lousy pool player. Larson, however, had the perfect look. All Campbell needed to do was find another officer, a bit younger with the right pool skills. He went back to the precinct, and it didn't take him long to find the right person.

And he found him. Officer Wildron. He looked more like a wrestler than a policeman, and pool was his passion. Giving him a pool cue was like giving a maestro a baton.

CHAPTER III

Bob had learned over the years as a detective that one doesn't dismiss any clue, no matter how insignificant. So if a button with a pool table and a cue stick was found, it was a start.

There were two pool halls in town, in entirely different neighborhoods. Larson and Wildron were sent to both. At the first, in a neighborhood of primarily one family homes and mostly residential, the majority of residents were older, retired persons. It sure didn't look like a place where criminals abounded. Nonetheless, in civilian attire and acting entirely unlike policemen, the two officers stepped inside. Here it seemed pretty orderly and civil. There was also a bar and outdoor veranda. Looked more like a country club. No one looked criminal or shady, and the patrons hardly noticed two men who had never been there before. From the moment they entered, to their walk past the bar and out to the veranda, they drew little attention. Nothing seemed amiss, the place was clean and proper, nor did anyone there appear to be the kind to run afoul of the law. The officers pretended to have a drink and left.

The second pool hall had a completely different ambience. Here, a much younger, more urban, disorderly crowd. Smoke filled the hall, beer bottles were everywhere, foul language abounded, some of the patrons belligerent. The appearance of the two officers drew immediate attention, and almost a total hush ensued. Officers Larson and Wildron recognized that more than just pool took place here. This was a lion's den. But as unfamiliar as Larson was with this environment, Wildron fit right in.

To avoid giving anyone the impression that they were police, the officers quickly adapted their speech, walk and demeanor. Wildron knew exactly how to behave, and Larson followed his example. It only took a while, but gradually the curiosity of the crowd diminished. Wildron was at home here, and he lit a cigarette. The crowd saw it, so any suspicions as to who these newcomers were faded.

If Larson and Wildron were going to check out any of the tough guys here, they had to be tough guys themselves. So they found a pool table, and with Wildron leading the way, prepping like a pro, they played a game. They were pretty good, and the crowd saw that Wildron was no amateur. They quickly got the attention of the crowd and were challenged to a game.

Nearly three hours and five games went by when, in the middle of a game, someone came in who caught the officer's attention at once. A man, early 30s, hair disheveled, pants ripped, shirt not tucked in. He was wearing a jacket with a series of buttons with a pool table and cue on them.   One button was missing.

Larson and Wildron looked at each other and gave a facial signal that this man might know something about the last robbery. Experienced detectives know how to start a conversation with a stranger, but first they had to watch him.

They played a game while observing closely. This stranger spoke to just a few people, he was neither open nor casual. He paid more attention to beers than anyone in particular. The officers heard some players call him Atom. That was strange, he wasn't small, but of average height and build. They'd soon learn how the name originated.

Someone gave Atom another beer, after which he seemed to relax. He was looking to play a game. The officers offered to play with him, and he accepted. They played two games.

Wildron bought Atom yet another beer and they went outside to talk. Small talk first, then a little sports and music. Larson asked him about the missing button.

Atom hesitated, looked to one side, took a sip of beer, and seemed ready to speak.

"It came off somewhere. I'm not sure where". Atom heard a song he liked coming from the lounge, he moved to the music, and finished the beer. By then he was in no condition to walk home. The officers drove him.

It was just a short ride. Arriving at the address, Larson and Wildron noticed that the atmosphere and condition of the building was a bit better than what they expected. Officer Wildron escorted Atom to the apartment on the second floor. Wildron made a note of the apartment number, Atom carefully opened the door to the apartment, not very much, as if to keep his newly found friend from seeing inside. Then he slinked inside and closed the door.

CHAPTER IV

The next day Officer Larson and Officer Al Lopez arrived with a search warrant. But it was not Atom who opened the door. An older man, mid 50s, but with a likewise unkempt look. He didn't seem to be too happy to find two police officers at this door.

"What you guys doin' here?" A pause. "I didn't call police."

Kevin Larson explained that the night before Atom was taken to this apartment, and they had some questions.

"Nobody else here."

Then in the background Atom appeared.

"Go back to bed, Eddie."

"Is his name Atom?"

Atom immediately recognized Larson. By now he was sober, alert, neater in appearance.

"That's alright, Broadway, he's one of the officers who took me home last night.

The officers entered and showed a photo of the button with the pool cue. Both Atom and Broadway got tense, the latter almost ready to push the officers out.

"We're going to look around."

The apartment was pretty well maintained, despite clothing spread around and dishes piled in the sink.

Lopez went into the both bedrooms while Larson kept a close eye on the two men. In the larger bedroom was found a drawer of jewelry, much of it women's. There was a fur, a coin collection, pages from a stamp album, old vinyl records, a few wads of cash, and some gold-plated figurines.

After a few minutes Lopez emerged.

"That's some pretty valuable stuff. Are you guys collectors?"

Lopez called for backup. In one minute two other policemen came in, while Larson and Lopez went back into the bedroom to collect the stolen goods. Some of it matched exactly the description of Edith's missing property. Others were items stolen in earlier robberies. Initials on some items and others were precisely what victims reported missing. The two men were arrested, taken into custody.

When taken to the police station, Broadway and Atom were interrogated separately. Broadway was really Peter, a man with a criminal record who had spent time in prison. He never worked a day in his life. A career criminal, he was able to live so well by stealing items of value, shaking people down and drug deals.

Atom was a different case altogether. Humble, cooperative, sorry for his crimes, he spoke almost the whole time with his head down.

His name was Steven Albus, and he had no family. A wanderer and vagrant, he had nowhere to go, no one to care for him. He met Broadway at the pool hall. Broadway bought him drinks and offered him a place to stay if Atom would steal.

Atom wasn't in favor of it but living on the streets he learned to survive. And how to rob. He paid attention to senior centers and followed members home. It didn't take long for him to know their schedules and how long they'd be gone. And thus he planned his crimes.

Officer Larson entered the room. Of all the police, Atom seemed to be most comfortable with this officer and most honest.

The officer offered Atom a drink. Atom said no. And the interrogation began.

"I'm really sorry for my crimes."

Larson saw that the regret was real. Atom didn't want to do any of them. He was almost in tears thinking how his victims felt when learning they had been robbed.

The topic switched to Broadway. Atom held him in awe but was also afraid of him.

"I've seen him get really rough with people. He can be very mean."

Atom admitted to being afraid of him. But he was more afraid of living on the streets.

"What about your family?", Officer Larson asked after a few minutes of silence.

Atom hesitated. For almost three minutes he was silent.

"Your Mom, Dad, brothers, sisters. Were you ever married?"

"I was never married." Again a long silence. "My Mom is dead. My father remarried. He moved somewhere out west. Haven't heard from him in years."

Silence. The room seemed to grow darker.

Officer Larson realized that this was emotional for Atom. He put a hand on the criminal's shoulder.

"Brothers, sisters?"

Atom looked up. "One of each. I haven't seen them in ages also."

"So how did you end up like this? Did you run away?"

Atom shook his head, looked up and down. Then he moved his arms to and from, stretching his neck, and he looked straight up.

"I ran away". A pause. "No, not really."

And once more a long silence. Except from this silence, Atom didn't look up.

Larson realized he wandered into sensitive territory. From years as a detective, he knew that criminals sometimes had their soft spots also. Obviously, he had reached that point with Atom.

Atom, real name Steven, got up and faced the wall. He looked at a framed photo on the desk. Pointed to it, then picked it up for a second, looked at it closely a few times. Then he put it down.

"You?" Atom inquired.

"Yes, when I was six years old".

Then Atom sat down, held back a tear, and looked at Officer Larson directly as if to say the story is about to begin.

CHAPTER V

After so many years as a detective, Kevin Larson heard all the stories one could imagine. Many of the criminals, especially the younger ones, came from broken families. Families where love, togetherness, education, and motivation were either in short supply or did not exist.

Larson also knew that when interrogating or interviewing suspects and criminals, that more than detective skills were needed. One often became a parent, sibling, psychologist, teacher, coach.

Some criminals are arrogant. Others get violent, lie, or insult. This wasn't Atom.

"What do you like to drink?" Officer Larson humbly asked.

"You got lemonade?" Atom replied.

The officer asked one of his assistants into the room. Handed him a couple of dollars, told the assistant to get a lemonade from the machine in the hall.

"Do you feel like talking?"

"Yes, I suppose."

The assistant brought in the lemonade.

"Thanks, Chris."

And Officer Larson proceeded with this suspect, as he did so many times before.

"So your name is Steven?'

"Yes."

"Where did the name Atom come from?"

"Broadway gave me the name. He thought I wasn't too smart if I was homeless, had no job and my life was a mess."

"Where are you from?"

"New Orleans."

"New Orleans? Don't they say N'orlins? You have no southern drawl."

"I only lived there until I was four. Then I moved to Philadelphia."

"Why the move?"

"My mother died when I was three. I loved her. But after she died, Dad got a girlfriend. He didn't care much for me."

"And your brother and sister?"

"I didn't have any. I'm an only child."

"But you said you had a brother and sister."

"They're my adopted brother and sister."

"Did your father remarry?"

"No. He took off with his girlfriend. I was left with an aunt and uncle. They were much older and their children were grown. They couldn't care for me. I don't blame them."

He paused. Put his head down, hands to his face, looked straight ahead. Then he continued.

"I lived with relatives, then was put in a foster home. Then up for adoption. A family named Albus outside of Philly adopted me. They had two children, also adopted."

Larson sat stone cold and speechless.

And Atom, also known as Steven Albus, resumed his life story. "Suddenly I had a new family, new home, new name."

"How old were you?"

"Four."

"And you got a new name?"

"Yes. Steven Albus."

"Your name before that?"

"I don't know. Zaszek or something like that. My adopted parents were never told. But my father saw it on one of the legal papers, just for a second."

"Did you ever hear from your father again?"

"No, never."

"Your aunt and uncle?"

"No, never from them either."

"Do you know where your mother is buried?"

"No, I don't know if there was a funeral or anything like that."

Larson had to address him more formally. He could see that the name Atom was childish. "Mind if I call you Steven?"

"No, that's my name."

"Why did your friend call you Eddie?"

"Broadway did that in public so people wouldn't get the idea I was being used by him to steal. At home I was Atom. In public I was Eddie."

Atom seemed to be more comfortable being called Steven.

"When did you meet Broadway?"

"Three years ago. I had no home. Was staying at Ys and shelters. I'd go play pool and that's where we met."

Officer Lopez entered and presented a rap sheet on Broadway. Larson carefully looked at it.

Lopez was next to speak. "Do you know who Peter Winters is?"

"Yeah, that's Broadway."

Lopez held out the papers. "He's got a rap sheet a mile long. Robbery, grand larceny, auto theft, rape. You know about this?"

"Of course I do."

Lopez asked, "And did you ever report it, or go to the police?"

"No." A long silence. "I couldn't."

"Why?"

"Broadway would have thrown me out. Or more likely have gotten a bunch of guys to murder me. I couldn't."

At this point Steven went to a window where he heard some children playing in a park next to the police station.

"I couldn't. I had nowhere to go. Those children, there, in that playground. They have a place to go. They have parents. They have family. I didn't. I had no one. Broadway gave me a place to stay and so I did what he asked. I didn't like it but had nowhere to go. No job, no family, no money."

He broke into tears.

CHAPTER VI

Steven Albus spent three weeks in prison when he was called into the warden's office. Officers Larson and Lopez were present also.

Steven was happy to see the officers, especially Larson, whom he was most comfortable with. Larson did the talking.

"Steven, Broadway is going to trial and facing a long list of charges. You have more knowledge of his crimes and motives than anyone else. The district attorney is offering you a deal."

Steven looked up curiously.

Officer Larson continued. "If you're willing to testify against him, the district attorney will give you immunity."

"Immunity?"

"The charges against you will be dropped. You won't go to trial, and you won't face any prison time."

Steven looked like for just a few seconds he was in another world. Then a smile.

"I'll do it!"

CHAPTER VII

Steven Albus was given a court appointed attorney. But it wasn't the real issue. His willingness to cooperate, avoid jail time and straighten out his life was the motivation he needed.

But the attorney told Steven that the trial wasn't going to be as easy as it seemed. Steven did have a criminal record and there was plenty of evidence to prove it. The defense attorney was going to cross-examine him and grill him hard. He had to be prepared for it.

His attorney was Jared Waller, a tall, thin athletic man one year older with a fondness for bow ties. They shared many of the same interests in music, sports, and movies. They began a preparation for a trial which, despite immunity, was going to be a chore for Steven. He'd be referred to as Atom, a past he wanted to put behind him.

Diligently, painstakingly, scrupulously they prepared for trial. Nearly every single day they covered each aspect of not only Broadway's crimes, but Atom's willing participation and role as accomplice.

A date was set for trial to begin. In the days leading up to it, attorney and client rehearsed like stage performers. Steven cut his hair, got fitted for professional clothes, and practiced proper English.

Broadway named him Atom, thinking his crime partner wasn't very bright. And Atom, alias Steven, had his first opportunity to be someone he had never been before. Each was soon to get shocks they never dreamed of.

CHAPTER VIII

Day one of the trial. Officers Kevin Larson, Al Lopez, and Chief Detective Robert Campbell were in court.

The first witnesses called by the prosecution were robbery victims whose possessions were returned. Another was a woman whom Broadway attempted to rape, and several whom he threatened to kill if he wasn't given money. Detectives testified to show that fingerprints at the crime scene were his.

Then Steven, also known as Eddie and Atom, took the stand as the star witness. Waller prepared him meticulously and cautiously. Steven took the oath.

"Can you tell the court your name, please?" Waller began.

"Steven Albus."

"Have you ever been known by any other names?"

"Yes."

"What are they?"

"Eddie, Atom."

"Who gave you these names?"

"Broadway"

"Why did he call you Eddie?"

"That was so anyone listening would not know me by my real name. It was only in public."

"Why did he name you Atom?"

"He said I was a jerk with a brain the size of an atom."

"Have you ever had any other name?"

"Yes, my birth name."

"What is it?"

"I'm not positive. Zaszek or something like that."

"Can you spell it please?"

"Z-A-S-Z-E-K"

"Why didn't you keep the name?"

"When I was adopted my new family's name became mine."

Steven spent quite a long time on the stand. Speaking intelligently, eloquently, professionally. He smoothly portrayed himself as nothing like the criminal or helpless servant to Broadway he once was.

But what he said after giving his birth name was lost on Officer Campbell. It was the precise second that Steven gave his birth name as Zaszek that a chord was struck in the chief police detective. He didn't know what it was. So mesmerized was Campbell by sound of the name Zaszek that he didn't notice how sentimental and emotional Steven got when discussing his birth name, especially his mother.

The testimony continued, but all Campbell could do at the time was lapse into a trance, because he knew he'd seen that name before.

By the end of cross-examination by the defense attorney, the subject of Steven's names was becoming a big target. The defense strategy was to make it appear Steven was irresponsible, a freeloader, using aliases and identities in attempts to deceive the law.

The defense hammered at him.

"Why have you had so many names? Are you trying to have more than one identity to avoid being captured?"

"No, I just accepted the names Broadway gave me." Silence, a glance to the side. "Sort of like nicknames."

And defense lawyer Gregoire pounded him further. "You expect this court to believe your testimony when you've had four names?"

Steven was ready. "I never used them legally. Only as Steven Albus."

"Do you expect this court to believe that you had but one legal name? Aren't you hiding something?"

Steven was as unflustered as a field of wildflowers. "I'm not hiding anything. I don't know my given birth name. I was so young when I was adopted."

Up to this point Steven had remained fairly calm, only losing some composure when discussing his mother. When he did, he showed a human side, not a harsh, lawless villain. But Gregoire pursued the subject of adoption and Steven's birth parents. As he did, the effects of emotion got the best of him. Steven was not just emotional, but tearful. The issue of the names, irresponsibility, aliases, came up over and over again despite the prosecution's objections.

Gregoire tried to portray it all as a hoax and a story to distract attention of Steven's guilt and willingness to be an accomplice. Deliberately he used different names when referring to different stages in the witness's life, misquoting the age of adoption, saying his birth name differently. It was all an attempt to confuse and blow holes in the testimony. But it did not seem to be working. Each time Steven corrected him. It not only showed intelligence but that his memory was still sharp as he accurately recalled names, dates, places. The jury was watching a man who couldn't be confounded. He was unflappable.

If there was any confusion, it was Officer Campbell. Each time the birth name was spoken, he knew that name was familiar.

Gregoire then turned his strategy towards the adoption. "You say that you were adopted?"

"Yes, I was."

"Where are your adopted parents?"

"I'm no longer in contact with them."

"So you don't know where they are?"

"I have no idea at all."

Gregoire tried a new path. "Could it be that you do know? And you just don't want this court to know that they kicked you out of their house?"

"That's not the case at all."

"Can you prove that you were adopted?"

"I have no papers, if that's what you mean."

"Have you a birth certificate?"

"No."

"So how do you expect us to believe that you know anything about Mr. Winters?" A pause as Gregoire planned this on the spot. "And what about your adopted family? Where are they?"

"I don't know" Steven said firmly.

"Mr. Albus, do you expect the court to believe this? You've gone by the names of Zaszek, Eddie, Atom, Steven." But it aroused no confusion in Steven. As Gregoire looked towards the jury, there didn't seem to be any faces that appeared undecided or puzzled.

The only puzzlement was with Campbell, who went deeper and deeper into thought, knowing that he saw or read or heard the name Zaszek before. He just didn't know where.

CHAPTER IX

As the trial went on, Campbell sat in the courtroom, his attention drifting from the testimony to where he heard the name Zaszek. His mind, attention, focus shifting to such a degree that at times he lost total track of the testimony and all cognizance of what was immediately around him.

When he was paying attention, he saw frames of testimony. Steven Albus claiming he was adopted, that Albus wasn't his birth name. The defense attorney calling it a fabrication, while Steven swearing it is all true. Steven remained calm, it raised sad emotions in a man who, it became more and more clear, was sentimental about the topic. Much as Gregoire tried to portray Steven as a heartless criminal, the opposite was happening.

Yet for reasons Campbell could not explain, he felt a connection.

Each day he went home, the uncertainty gnawed at him. Had he heard the name before, or was it his imagination?

He went home and asked his wife Donna. She could think of no one she ever knew with that name. Perhaps a neighbor they once had, or maybe one of her patients when she worked at a clinic in the early days of their marriage. Donna couldn't think of anyone. Still, she checked personal phone directories, old greeting cards, contact lists. No one with that name.

Then Bob Campbell turned to his two children. Maybe a former classmate, or someone once on their bowling team. With each successive dead end, he was more determined. He thought of people he knew from all parts of his past. That fat, 300-pound, unappealing judgmental guy who criticized everyone but himself. The crazy woman at the church who directed plays, flirted with men and none showed her any interest. The former coworker who liked trivia games.

Maybe a character from a film. Bob is a movie fan, saw hundreds of films, but couldn't think of any. So he went to his basement and took out the old film glossary. Checking it scrupulously, it produced nothing.

He didn't give up. Photo albums, class pictures, school yearbooks, classmates at the police academy. Then he had his children check their photo albums, class pictures and yearbooks.

Then the trial took a surprise turn. Gregoire stated that the lack of birth certificate and legal papers made the adoption seem unlikely. For the first time, Gregoire was making progress. Was the adoption allegation just an attempt to elicit sympathy and had no reality?

For the first time Steven got excited. He stood up from his seat in the witness stand, leaned towards Gregoire, and for the first time raised his voice. It was just what the defense wanted so late in the trial. The jurors were certain to remember such behavior and make it indicative of how a criminal behaves.

"Ladies and gentlemen of the jury, perhaps now the true character comes out. Up until now this witness has just been an actor, showing himself to be a waif, a victim, downtrodden by society. But now you have seen it. He is capable of anti-social behavior, of being irate, of anger and using it against helpless victims. He was not adopted; he's just using that to get sympathy. I urge you to reject his testimony and see him as the criminal he really is. He was not an accomplice; it was he who led Mr. Winters into committing crimes."

Day after day, Bob Campbell thought of the name Zaszek. He checked all his school yearbooks and class pictures again and again. At his job he checked all police records, criminal files, names of witnesses and police officers. Couldn't find anything.

He knew it was not right, but he checked motor vehicle records and old telephone directories. Nothing.

Back and forth he went to court, hoping something would give him a clue as to where he heard the defendant's birth name. With the trial winding down, he realized to himself that maybe it was all just a mirage and he never really knew the name at all.

So one Friday afternoon, he left the police station. Encountering traffic, he took another route home, where he passed a ballfield and there were two teams playing a lively game. For a split second he remembered that was just what he did decades ago. Campbell stopped for a traffic light, and saw a ball someone hit go straight to the fence and land in front of a stone along the side of the concrete seats.

It was a sweaty, steamy and humid night, he arrived home tired, and took a nap while Donna was preparing dinner. And as he drifted off to a short sleep, the image of the ball he saw come to a stop in front of a stone on his way home from the police station transformed into that equally hot summer day so many years before when he was a young boy and hit a fly ball into the cemetery.   At that very moment he woke up and remembered clearly where he where first saw the name Zaszek.

CHAPTER X

It was Friday afternoon and court was not in session for the weekend. The trial was nearing an end, and Steven Albus' credibility had been somewhat shattered by the defense attorney who shot holes in his adoption story.

Campbell had just days to act. He knew where that old cemetery was located. He didn't know its name or who managed it. But there was no time to waste. He did some research on his computer. With a little effort he learned the name, but not anyone who operated it nor of any office where records of the deceased were maintained. Nor was there any guarantee that someone named Zaszek buried in that graveyard was any relation to Steven Albus. But he had to give it all he had. Time was running out and he owed it to a witness who was testifying on the law's behalf. Campbell's position as a chief of detectives gave him an advantage he was going to use.

He had the weekend off, but early the next morning he was at his office. Instantly he got on the telephone with the police department of the county he grew up in. It took a few calls, but eventually he got the name of the groundskeeper who knew where the official records were kept. The office would not be open until Monday. That was no problem. It gave him time to call the prosecutor.

"Jared, I'm not saying this will blow the court away, but I may have some information that will save Albus."

"What do you mean" Waller asked, more than curiously.

"The name Zaszek - I've got some information on it. It may be a long shot, but we've got to take the chance." Campbell explained it all.

"By all means, go ahead" Waller ordered.

"I'll get the warrant. This is too important to delay."

Early Monday morning, before sunrise, Campbell was in his car and on his way to the office where he would meet the groundskeeper. Donna went with him.

It was just a short ride from that old, seldom visited cemetery. On his way to the office, he passed the graveyard, parked his car, and for a very brief time looked around. His wife with him, he gazed with wonder and astonishment at the exact same place where 52 years before he played ball. It was all still there. The ballfield, the bleacher stands, the cemetery, the wrought iron fence. As he studied them all, it seemed almost surreal that the ballfield and bleachers had changed more than the graveyard. The ballfield itself was well manicured, with clear baselines. The bleacher stands were also in tiptop shape. They weren't the same bleachers he remembered. These looked to be fairly new. Good condition, plus water fountains, a barbecue pit. There were shrubs and bushes along the edges of the property that were not present when he played.

And then he looked at the cemetery. It seemed to be precisely as it was when he last saw it. Overrun with weeds, vines, unpruned trees and what looked like a muskrat or prairie dog scampering along the ground. Only one grave had some kind of memorial to indicate a recent visit by a loved one. All the rest were bare, no flowers, wreaths, or decorations. It appeared almost mysterious that when he went to the ballfield he heard echoes of games once played, fans cheering, people calling out for a cold drink or a sandwich. He felt the wind blow and a slight whistle of a gust. Then he walked to the perimeter of the cemetery, and dead silence. There didn't seem to be any wind, not the slightest breeze.

They arrived at the cemetery office, explained the case to the groundskeeper. It was a very small, crowded office, not much more than a tiny room. The clerk, a man appearing to be in his late sixties, acted like he was expecting them. They exchanged no more than a dozen words, as the office clerk smiled and presented to them the information they requested.

The papers were obviously old, covered with a thick plastic shield for protection, and in remarkably good condition. Studying the death certificate and additional papers, it stated that Maria Zaszek had two children. Their names and addresses at the time of death were shown, both near to the graveyard. It was now or never. Campbell knew there was no time to waste. He called one child; Donna called the other.

Donna called the first name, that of a son. No one answered.

Then Campbell called daughter Connie Zaszek. A woman greeted a soft hello. Campbell explained what he was calling about. For a few seconds Connie thought it was someone joking. Then he gave the date of birth of Steven and a description.

"Could he be a relative of yours?"

A gasp.

"That's my son!" Campbell could feel her excitement, hear her tears.

She didn't live far away. It wasn't yet noon when Bob and Donna got to Connie Zaszek' s house and explained fully the whole case. "And that's the whole thing", Bob and Connie said almost in unison.

Then later that afternoon, just after court was adjourned for the day, Campbell called Waller. "Jared, I've got the best news in the world!"

The next morning in the courtroom Jared Waller announced that he had one more witness to call.

"The prosecution calls Connie Zaszek."

CHAPTER XI

As Connie Zaszek entered the witness box, the entire court was spellbound. No one more so than Steven Albus.

Connie looked at Steven in a way no one else had ever done before. She had yet to utter one word, and Steven looked at her without blinking an eye. He knew this was going to be the most emotional and poignant day of his life.

It seemed like an eternity, but Connie was now in the witness stand and her testimony began.

Waller asked, "Tell the court your name and where you live."

"Connie Zaszek", giving her address. Steven was both smiling and crying.

"Do you have any children?"

"Yes, a son. I gave him up for adoption when he was four years old."

"Why did you do that?"

"I could no longer care for him. I didn't want him to grow up feeling his mother abandoned him or that his father left us. So I sent him to my sister and brother-in-law. They had two older children. They didn't have the money or stamina to care for him. So they decided to put him up for adoption."

"Did you know about this?"

Connie was near tears. "I knew that they were considering adoption. They asked me to take him back, but I couldn't. I told them to wait, give me a little more time. But it wasn't possible. I didn't want any more to do with it".

"When did you learn of the adoption?"

"Not until many years later". Tears were streaming down her face.

"Do you know who the man sitting next to my assistant is?"

"Yes, he is my son."

The testimony continued a bit longer. When it concluded, Connie Zaszek asked if she could hug her son. The judge allowed it. It was a moment neither one of them ever thought would happen.

That ended the testimony.

The jury deliberated for four hours and returned a guilty verdict against Peter Winters. A criminal was taken off the streets. Crime victims got their property back. But the real winner was a man who would soon be known as Steven Zaszek. He got his name, family, freedom and dignity back. All made possible by Detective Campbell and a foul ball he hit into a cemetery over half a century before. A foul ball which turned into the greatest home run he ever hit.